A Note to Parents

The *Dorling Kindersley Readers* series is a reading program for children which is highly respected by teachers and educators around the world. The LEGO Company has a global reputation for offering high-quality, innovative products, specially designed to stimulate a child's creativity and development through play.

Now Dorling Kindersley has joined forces with The LEGO Company to produce the first-ever graded reading program to be based around LEGO play themes. Each *Dorling Kindersley Reader* is guaranteed to capture a child's imagination, while developing his or her reading skills, general knowledge, and love of reading.

The books are written and designed in conjunction with literacy experts, including Dr. Linda Gambrell, President of the National Reading Conference and past board member of the International Reading Association.

The four levels of *Dorling Kindersley Readers* are aimed at different reading abilities, enabling you to choose the books that are right for each child.

Level 1 – for Preschool to Grade 1
Level 2 – for Grades 1 to 3
Level 3 – for Grades 2 and 3
Level 4 – for Grades 2 to 4

The "normal" age at which a child begins to read can be from three to eight years old, so these levels are only guidelines.

Dorling Kindersley

LONDON, NEW YORK, SYDNEY, DELHI, PARIS,
MUNICH and JOHANNESBURG

Senior Editor Cynthia O'Neill
Senior Art Editor Nick Avery
Senior Managing Editor Karen Dolan
Managing Art Editor Cathy Tincknell
DTP Designer Jill Bunyan
Production Chris Avgherinos
US Editor Gary Werner

Reading Consultant
Linda B. Gambrell, Ph.D

First American Edition, 2000
6 8 10 9 7 5
Published in the United States by Dorling Kindersley Publishing, Inc.
95 Madison Avenue, New York, New York 10016

© 2000 The LEGO Company
® LEGO is a registered trademark belonging to The LEGO Company
and used here by special permission.

www.lego.com

Library of Congress Cataloging-in-Publication Data
Birkinshaw, Marie
Trouble at the bridge / by Marie Birkinshaw. – 1st American ed
p. cm. (Dorling Kindersley Readers)
Summary: as the LEGO city builders hurry to complete a new bridge, they
face an unusual problem when a bank robber tries to hide in their giant crane.
ISBN 0-7894-6093-9 (hardcover) 0-7894-5457-2 (pb)
[1. Bridges--Fiction. 2. Robbers and outlaws --Fiction.] I.Title. II.Series.

P27.B5225 Tr2000
[Fic}--dc21
99-053094

Color reproduction by Dot Gradations, UK
Printed and bound by L Rex, China

www.dk.com

DORLING KINDERSLEY *READERS*

Trouble at the
Bridge

Written by Marie Birkinshaw • Illustrated by Sebastian Quigley

Level 1 PRESCHOOL-GRADE 1

A Dorling Kindersley Book

The LEGO City Builders
were building a new bridge.

They had to finish it
by the next day.

"We must work all night,"
Builder Pete told his crew.

Shades was shifting the rubble in the big digger.

Hardhat Jones
took the rubble away
in his dump truck.

That evening,
Highway Patrolman Bill arrived.

"I will close the road to traffic,"
he told Builder Pete.

"Then your crew
can finish the bridge safely –
it will be dark soon."

That night, the Brickster
was hiding in the dark
outside the LEGO City Bank.

The Brickster was
a bank robber.

He broke into the bank and
stole all the money.

Brrrng!
Brrrng!
Brrrng!

The Brickster set off the alarm!

Brrrng!
Brrrng!
Brrrng!

He made
a quick
getaway.

He went to the new bridge.
"Nobody will look for me here,"
laughed the Brickster.

Highway Patrolman Bill
heard the alarm.
He hurried to the bank
but he could not find
the Brickster.

The Brickster was hiding
inside a crane bucket!

The LEGO City Builders
had worked all night.

"Nearly finished!"
said Hardhat Jones
the next morning.
He went to get the
concrete mixer.

Shades climbed into
the crane cab.
He lifted the bucket
into the air.

But then the crane broke down.
The bucket would not move.

"Listen!" shouted Builder Pete.
"I think I can
hear someone!"

Everyone stopped to listen.

"Help!" called the Brickster.
He was up in the crane bucket
and he could not get down.

The builders called
the fire crew.

The fire crew had to hurry –
the builders had to finish
the bridge that day.

The fire crew arrived
at top speed.
The firefighters used
the fire truck,
with its long ladders.

The Brickster
was too scared
to move.

Firefighter Jack
called for the helicopter.

"We must use the winch
on the helicopter," he said.
"That will get him down safely."

Everyone watched the rescue.

The firefighters carried
the Brickster down.
He was still holding
the money.

"You won't get away again!"
said Highway Patrolman Bill.

"I am taking you to jail,"
he told the Brickster.

The LEGO City Builders
fixed the crane.
Then they started
work again.
They put the last piece
of bridge in place.

At last, the bridge
was finished.

Now the cars could use
the road <u>and</u> the bridge.

The builders climbed
into the truck.

"That Brickster won't make trouble at this bridge for a long time!" smiled Shades. Then the builders drove home for a long sleep!

What do they do?

Trucks
carry heavy loads.
They are strong,
with big wheels.

Patrol trucks
carry road signs
so that police officers
can direct the traffic.

Diggers
|bucket

scrape up dirt
in their buckets
to make big holes.

Dump trucks
carry dirt and stones
away from the
building site.